With best regards,

Arun Kumar Pallathadka

The Broken Spear - 1800 BCE
History - War - Love

JustFiction Edition

Impressum / Imprint
Bibliografische Information der Deutschen Nationalbibliothek: Die Deutsche Nationalbibliothek verzeichnet diese Publikation in der Deutschen Nationalbibliografie; detaillierte bibliografische Daten sind im Internet über http://dnb.d-nb.de abrufbar.
Alle in diesem Buch genannten Marken und Produktnamen unterliegen warenzeichen-, marken- oder patentrechtlichem Schutz bzw. sind Warenzeichen oder eingetragene Warenzeichen der jeweiligen Inhaber. Die Wiedergabe von Marken, Produktnamen, Gebrauchsnamen, Handelsnamen, Warenbezeichnungen u.s.w. in diesem Werk berechtigt auch ohne besondere Kennzeichnung nicht zu der Annahme, dass solche Namen im Sinne der Warenzeichen- und Markenschutzgesetzgebung als frei zu betrachten wären und daher von jedermann benutzt werden dürften.

Bibliographic information published by the Deutsche Nationalbibliothek: The Deutsche Nationalbibliothek lists this publication in the Deutsche Nationalbibliografie; detailed bibliographic data are available in the Internet at http://dnb.d-nb.de.
Any brand names and product names mentioned in this book are subject to trademark, brand or patent protection and are trademarks or registered trademarks of their respective holders. The use of brand names, product names, common names, trade names, product descriptions etc. even without a particular marking in this works is in no way to be construed to mean that such names may be regarded as unrestricted in respect of trademark and brand protection legislation and could thus be used by anyone.

Coverbild / Cover image: www.ingimage.com

Verlag / Publisher:
JustFiction! Edition
ist ein Imprint der / is a trademark of
OmniScriptum GmbH & Co. KG
Heinrich-Böcking-Str. 6-8, 66121 Saarbrücken, Deutschland / Germany
Email: info@justfiction-edition.com

Herstellung: siehe letzte Seite /
Printed at: see last page
ISBN: 978-3-8454-4999-9

Copyright © 2013 OmniScriptum GmbH & Co. KG
Alle Rechte vorbehalten. / All rights reserved. Saarbrücken 2013

THE BROKEN SPEAR
-1800 BCE-

ARUN KUMAR PALLATHADKA

Acknowledgements

My inspiration to write a book is my father. Although he was not an established writer in that sense as one would understand, he still possessed a great style of writing that was all his own.

Many more people are explicitly connected to the writing of this book; many more implicitly. Above all, I'm happy to thank Dr. Rohitha Eshwer, Archaeologist and Professor at University of Mysore, for archaeological discussions and other guidance.

I can't thank enough Professor Dr. Vasant Shinde who has contributed his valuable time to write foreword for this book.

My family has been very supportive and I thank them for the same.

I gracefully acknowledge my sincere gratitude to Mr. Prakash Shetty, the renowned caricaturist and my good friend, who prepared drawings for this work.

Last but not least, I thank *JustFiction! Edition* Publications for agreeing to publish and distribute this book.

Any misinterpretations or errors in the narrative remain my sole responsibility.

Arun Kumar Pallathadka

Table of Contents

Foreword	5
Preface by the Author	8
Introduction	9
Chapter I	11
Chapter II	23
Chapter III	30
Chapter IV	46
Chapter V	56
Chapter VI	64
Chapter VII	70
Bottom Line	81
Taking it Further	82

Foreword

Mr. Arun Kumar Pallathadka has presented to the readers a beautiful novel "*The Broken Spear- 1800 BCE*" based on actual evidence from some of the excavated Harappan sites that flourished in the northwest part of the Indian subcontinent almost five thousand years ago. This is one of the best writings that I have come across by an Indian based on actual archaeological data. I, in the beginning of my academic career as an archaeologist, had a chance to read similar novel titled "*The Source*", which was immensely popular and was a wonderful work based on archaeological finds. I immensely developed interest in the subject after reading that novel. I wish to narrate a very interesting encounter with a very powerful minister of Maharashtra, who visited our University sometime back. He was shown and explained the archaeological collection exhibited in our Museum, but at the end he said since such subjects are of no use, they should not be taught in Universities. We do not blame such a layperson for such a reaction as this reflects our failure to take this subject to the masses and explain them what we learn from it and its utility and significance to the modern world. We have immensely rich cultural heritage and traditional knowledge system, which has contributed substantially to the history of South Asia and the world. The technological and cultural base of South Asia lies in the Harappan Civilization. Without understanding its roots, we will not understand the present and future. This is the Civilization of the entire mankind and cannot be claimed by any narrow-minded religious group.

In order to popularize subjects like Archaeology, special efforts must be made and one of them could be to produce popular writings of such a quality. The subject needs to be presented in a very lucid and simple form and not in technical and jargon language. This is exactly what Mr. Pallathadka has done. He has presented the entire history of the Harappan Civilization in a form of a story. It is well known, on the basis of evidence, that there were a few contemporary communities living around the Harappan Civilization. The Harappans established cordial relationship with them for their posterity and development. In this novel the author has shown a tussle between two communities for supremacy over the region and technology. The archaeological evidence from this period indeed demonstrates that the Harappans had interactions with their contemporaries living on all four directions. This interaction according to most of the scholars was established to facilitate acquisition of raw material and distribution of finished goods and technology. This interaction enabled them and their contemporaries to exchange ideas and cultural elements and attain prosperity. Arun has presented these important facets of the Early Civilization in a story form and this will be indeed appreciated by one and all. The common people will not only understand history but will surely develop more interest in such writings. More and more such writings should exist so that the subject does not remain dry and beyond the perception of the common people and students.

There is no significant evidence of the fight between two communities during the Harappan times. There is hardly any evidence about the existence of the Aryans and non-Aryans some five thousand years ago in the Indian subcontinent. But in order to make interesting reading the author has provided this event, which goes well with the theme of the novel. The description of their life-style, dress patterns, ornaments, tools, religious beliefs, philosophical thinking, etc. is real and in tune with the evidence unearthed from many Harappan sites in the Indian subcontinent. The decline and the end of the Harappan culture are not correctly understood yet. Factors like drying up of the climatic conditions leading to the abandonment of agricultural bases, drying up of the major river Saraswati, decline of international trade due to lowering of sea level, breaking up of the social set up, etc. could have led to the decline and end of the Harappan Civilization. The surviving people began to migrate to the periphery area and got merged with the local non-Harappan population. However, most of the traditions, technological and scientific developments started in this period were carried forward and have survived until the modern times. The northwest part of the subcontinent still boasts of continuing Harappan tradition. It is true that the Harappan cultural elements have vanished but its legacy has continued until today.

Arun has created a wonderful work and I vouch it will be liked by all. This will serve to popularize this subject and I wish many more such writings should be undertaken. The readers will be desperate to welcome this lovely new literary piece. After reading this novel, people will expect many more such writings from Arun and I am confident he will fulfill their expectations. Arun deserves heartiest congratulations for choosing such a difficult theme and making it very interesting.

Professor Vasant Shinde
Senior Archaeologist / Joint Director
Deccan College, Pune, India
Post-Graduate and Research Institute (Deemed University)

Preface by the Author

History is more than what we study. However, the question as to how many of us really love studying history is a matter of debate. A reasonable answer would be a 'countable' number, indeed. People often see history as a passive subject and take it for granted. What we don't realize is that it is where our past lies. History is made by our forefathers' lives and it is certainly not without their contributions. Therefore, History is not without them offering us lessons. History is more than what we study. That is why I would like to mention - call my work a story, an essay or a thesis. It makes no difference. This is an attempt to throw light on some of the aspects related to the cultural, social and religious life of the Harappan people. Of course, it is not possible to write a book on Harappan Culture in a month or two. Any study on Harappan Culture will keep an Archaeologist, whether professional or amateur, engaged with the subject matter for several years. My intention here is to present my readers with an idea about how people lived in ancient times. This is a historic fiction, referring to the story. The Harappan and Aryan cultures presented here are subject to further reading and examination. However, they are precise and accurate to the best of my knowledge. This story is based on the assumption that Aryan invasion has taken place at some point of time and is responsible for the downfall of the Harappan Culture.

Remember, this is not an encyclopedia on Harappan culture. Don't expect to find everything you want to know about Harappan Culture, because I do not set out to present a comprehensive guide on the topic. The books listed in the 'taking it further' section will do that – but if you read what I have written, I hope that you will be inclined to take matters further.

Arun Kumar Pallathadka

Introduction

History tells us that people of ancient times often engaged in armed conflicts for various reasons. Yet there is not even the slightest clue about what might be the exact issues, though Archaeologists assume and suggest infinite possibilities. Man's greed for land, wealth and woman is long known and has a recorded history over two millennia. The following story is no different. History is all about exposing the mistakes that occurred in the past due to the misdeeds of our forefathers and correcting those misdeeds from time to time.

About seven thousand years before the start of current era (what is generally referred to as 1 AD), there lived plenty of peaceful communities across the modern day continents. There was no place for mass violence in any culture. War was not a part of any culture; therefore, it had been considered the last possibility. People had a loving understanding of nature in which they had been brought up. This very loving concern made them work hard. The revolution in agriculture, especially those days, required people to settle down. Soon they started to build towns and this is probably how the major civilizations have come into existence. Obviously, rivers have played a major role in almost all the civilizations that flourished once. When the towns grew bigger and bigger, people began to think that they had become too rich to engage in work anymore. Like they say, an idle mind produces evil thoughts; it was similar with our ancient cultures. Thus we realize the most important fact - It was only with time that people began to think about war, bloodshed and death. The reason was to accumulate wealth. Wealth blindfolded man in such a way that it was no longer a healthy approach. It was only for wealth, be it land, gold or women.

Migrations made man to adapt different environments. Early invasions were actually human migrations in search of better livelihood. Later, as we understand, one civilization started to conquer the other for supremacy, which included all aspects connected to human life. Eventually, it was man's greed for these which brought about his own destruction. Man became the architect of his own misfortune. All through our history, what our mankind has been doing is quite the same. And we really wonder how can a man do it and then live, without any regret?! Only within the context of time can this question be answered.

ಞ

CHAPTER I

The dawn broke early in the valley of the great Indus river. Down the valley, people in the town of Daro welcomed the early rise of the Sun. They bowed and greeted Him reverently.

People who lived the by the Indus River went on to their fields to check the growth of the pulses. People, who breathed trade, began moving towards the granaries and warehouses. Fishermen were untying the ropes from the boats they had moored the previous night. The Priest initiated his daily worship sitting before the altar in the great citadel, which was situated in the middle of the town, built on a raised platform. There, he would take the bath in the stepped pool and conduct daily worship of Mother Goddess with a basket full of flowers and grains; every morning, he decorated the deity with handmade stone ornaments and wild flowers, which the folk offered him.

The priest was a tall-fat man with more or less fair, or what may be termed so, complexion; his mustache, stubbles beard and bulgy eyes gave him a fierce appearance.

The townsmen not only hurried themselves to work dragging their cattle, which they had successfully domesticated over the years.

While everyone in the town was in a hurry to make a move, there was a boy who was still in his bed, a bed which was made out of an animal skin tightly draped over a wooden frame; he thinking of the variety of fishes and jagged rocks his father was going to bring for him, later in the evening. He pulled his cotton blanket upon him sniffing the clay wall beside. He saw his mother preparing fried fish.

"Can I have a piece, Mother?" He asked hastily.

"Almighty first!" She warned him.

An hour later, the priest declared that the God's share had been accepted and accordingly, people could have their meals.

The lazy boy was called by the name- Ama. He had a dreamer's mind and always thought of himself undertaking an adventure like he had heard from father and mother.

His father collected materials from the river and traded them the next day. There was a complex system of trade networks. Ama's father traded in shell, dried fish, fish grain, and pearls from the coast, as well as precious and semi-precious stones from the hill country. Sumerians, Chinese, Central Asians, Mesopotamians, Egyptians and Arabs used to visit the town every month. He imagined how it would be like if he could travel with them to undertake great adventures.

Ama was amazed at how they could traverse from distant lands. He feared that sea monsters and valley beasts might hurt them on the way. He also wondered how people could cross the great mountains by foot. His father would not answer his delicate questions, but would always point his finger at the bright sun. His father believed that above all was the Sun.

Ama was considered asinine by his neighbors because he would carefully observe the night sky and ask why the stars twinkled, why they disappeared in the day, why the Moon died once in every fortnight and so on. His questions were rather complex and would have enraged the priest. If he had ever questioned the priest, the priest would have certainly punished him, by locking him up in the citadel for the first three days of new moon, without food and water.

Ama was a boy aged about thirteen years. He always used to sit by his parents to listen to their conversation, as it included discussions about the people who came from the farthest lands to purchase the Harappan goods. Ama fantasized about their long journey on foot, which he considered as the greatest adventure one could ever undertake.

"Why do we not go to faraway places? Why do we not move?" Ama asked innocently.

"Do you see that great Mountain in the North?" asked his mother.
"Yes."

"The vast sea in the west, you must have heard about it," she remarked.

"Of course!"

"Those are our boundaries as marked by Mother Goddess."

"Who says so?"

"The priest! None of us are entitled to go beyond these boundaries. We should not even think of it- think of crossing the boundaries. Not even for the sake of curiosity. The worst will happen."

"Who is Mother Goddess?"

"She reigns over this region, my son. She demands sacrifices. Without her blessing, no one can set off. She looks favorably upon us as far as we don't offend her."

"Where is she?"

"She is immensely powerful. You can feel the air around you. You can see the Sun above you. The tree, the mountains, the seas, the moon and so on, everything belongs to *Her*."

"Can we never move from this place?"

Ama asked seeing his mother in silence.

"Yes. But only towards Him!"

She pointed at the burning Sun through the square shaped window.

"He can lead you to a better place. He never deceives those who follow Him. Believe Him, not because you can see Him, but you can see everything because of Him. Should you move someday, move in the eastern direction, where the Sun takes his birth every morning. This is the proclamation of the priest," she said with an apparent inexpressible fear.

She worried that he might try to cross the boundary since he was too young to have common sense. So her voice trembled continuously. Ama did not really think of going beyond the great Mountains or sailing across the vast ocean, though, he fantasized, every now and then, himself undertaking one such journey, without any kind of fear, of neither his mother nor the holy priest.

"What is there in the eastern direction?" Ama mumbled. He could not understand why one should keep walking on the plain lands, of which his mother talked, that in which one could not find any elements of beauty.

"I wonder why!" Ama said unhappily.

He looked at the mighty sky-touching mountains in the North, and imagined the vast-blue Ocean in the west. He gasped saying, "I'm so unfortunate!"

It was a Full Moon day. All the townsmen had gathered around the citadel. Ama was standing behind his mother being nervous. The priest walked upstairs, held his sacred spear and spoke in a high tone,

"The Mother Goddess is highly pleased with the way things have been going on in the town! Yet she foresees an unusually realistic event to occur in the near future."

The news upset them in no time. The priest shut his eyes in order to read the future. Ama felt as though he had gone off.

The townsmen waited for at least a couple of hours to see the priest open his eyes again. The terracotta figurine which was there at the front of the platform seemed to have received the divine light from the moon.

"One boy in the town…," he stammered, "is destined to meet his fortune from the North. The Mother Goddess says he is thirteen at present!"

"Ah!" the townsmen sighed together.

"Should he be abandoned?" the servant of the priest voiced his opinion before the public.

"Mother Goddess is silent about what kind of fortune it is…"
The priest paused.

"More will be announced on the next Full Moon!"

The priest wrapped the ceremony up. As the townsmen moved, Ama wondered who that lucky boy was.

Ama's mother became tensed. She knew it was none other than her son whose future the Mother Goddess had foreseen. Presently, there were not more than a hundred children in the town. Among them, less than twenty were between ten and fifteen years of age. As a further matter, Ama was the one who looked up to the North. 'What would the priest do to my son?' She was afraid even to come to a conclusion.

On the contrary, Ama sat on the riverside, thinking about his oncoming fortune. He was all excited about it.

The next twenty nine days, there were strange signs around. The folk witnessed wildfires and landslides. No one could understand where the world was coming to. In the meantime, many went missing.

With a total of thirty days gone, another Full Moon arrived. The folk were anxious to hear about the oncoming hurdle. The priest looked mysterious and frightened. Ama moved back and forth, trying to hide himself somewhere behind his mother, so that he was safe from the eyes of the priest. The priest declared in a serious tone,

"Today, I address you not as the priest of Daro of Indus Valley, not as a learned scholar, not even as the messenger of Mother Goddess; but as a representative of humanity. This is my painful duty to inform you that one among us has crossed the boundaries without telling anything about it. He has gone against our norms. This is not a good sign at all. We have offended our Mother Goddess!

My dear townsmen, the day of verdict has come. The day of last battle is no longer in murk. It is about to arrive in a week or so. No one can stop it. Over the past two thousand years, we have rebuilt our towns over seven times. During every crisis, we have somehow managed to survive. But I'm afraid that's impossible this time. The Mother Goddess foretells that it is not the rage of any of her sons- sky, river, wind, earth and fire. This is something inexplicable. The danger is coming from the North- beyond the Mountains."

The priest took a deep breath,

"Follow the Sun, my townsmen. Go in the eastern direction. Those who ought to protect their town may remain. The rest may follow the Sun."

There was a long silence. The priest shouted,

"I may not speak to you again. Make your decision as quickly as possible. Defence or Migration?"

"Defence!" the crowd roared back.

Harappans were peace loving people. They hardly used any weapons although they possessed weapons like spear, axes made of stone and copper, tridents, arrow, bows and knives, mainly for domesticating animals. They had never engaged in an armed conflict before. They did not keep a well-trained troop. There was a group of town guards who were always on the watch. Apart from this small number of guards, there was nothing like an army to protect Harappan towns from external aggressions.

Future was uncertain, the happenings could not be challenged and they knew it very well. But they hoped that they could at least find solutions to minimize the risk.

For five days and nights, nobody in the town could sleep. Everyone was awaiting death. But none of them knew in which form it was going to come. Everyone was praying for the safety of his/her beloved ones. Those who worked in the farms became idle, traders became unenthusiastic; all of them set their cattle free. However, nothing really happened in those six days.

On the sixth night, the townsmen were deep asleep. They had already spent five nights with little or no sleep. The priest was uttering strange verses sitting before the altar.

Suddenly, a dusty wind blew across the town. As the owls cried, a comet moved ominously across the starry sky. They were seeing the warning signs that a danger was minutes away.

"They're coming! They're coming on four-legged strange looking creatures!" One of the town guards shouted from the gigantic doorway in the North.

CHAPTER II

The next morning, Ama found himself in a sitting position inside the hearth. His body had been covered with a woolen rug. He did not know why he had been placed inside the hearth and who had done it. He shivered and called his mother repeatedly. But there was no answer. He looked around. There was no one inside. He peeped through the window only to find the streets having been completely abandoned.

As he walked in the streets, he found the broad streets being unusually deserted. In spite of Harappan streets being as wide as seven feet, he could see nothing more than blood. There was blood everywhere. The brick houses were burning in fire.

Alas, the next street looked like a cemetery.

The dead bodies filled both sides of the streets. Many children had died. Many more had lost eyes and limbs. Ama's heart melted seeing the misery of his peer group. His father's co-workers were seen dead in front of their respective houses. The dead bodies of women were seen next to their husbands. The wounds on their bodies were deep and intense since those wounds must have been caused by the deep penetration of spears.

Ama walked further searching for his father and mother. He could see them nowhere. His heart began beating faster.

He reached a square where he saw his father and mother lying on the bloodshed brick pavement, all alone and motionless. Ama was shocked.

He couldn't believe what he was seeing. He shook the bodies of his father and mother again and again in order to bring them back to life.

"Father, wake up!" He cried, "Mother, talk to me."

Mother gained all her strength to speak her last words,

"Ama, I'm glad you are safe," she struggled to continue.

"An alien force has killed these innocent folk, Ama. Merciless people, they are…"

She sobbed.

"Listen to me, a few people have moved to the outskirts of the town. You must go there and join them immediately."

As a reaction, Ama looked towards his father. His father's neck was hurt. The veins below the neck were cut. Yet there was a spear in his hand. He had held it so tightly that the spear could not be separated from his hand, now. Then, he worked on to remove the spear from his father's hand. Surprisingly, it did not take much time. Ama held the spear in his hand and vowed revenge. His mother still tried to stop him,

"Throw it away, my son. Have no revenge because certain is the death for the born. Men rise and fall like winter crops. What remains is the name you achieve during the lifetime, through peace and service. These unnecessary conflicts are of no use. It only gets worse. Put an end to all this suffering. Put an end to this evil. Let this suffering cease with my death; with your father's death. Throw it away, Ama. Throw it away. It is…"

Ama shook his head in disagreement. She made forceful efforts to breathe, strived hard, and finally took her final breath. Her mouth was slightly open in a gesture of not being able to complete what she wanted to say.

The sky was no longer azure, but overcast. Soon it started raining. Deep inside his heart, he was burning. The rain could not suppress it, nor could his tears. Ama was a child until he saw his own people die before his eyes. Then he was not a child anymore; one incident had turned him into a sworn warrior, the pledge of defeating the slayers and establishing peace in the Indus river valley once again. Now that he had pledged, no once could change it. He had no idea, really, about what his vow meant. He had vowed something and that had come from the bottom of his heart. The last words of his mother still echoed in his ears, even though he allotted very less importance to what his mother said before she died.

The human values within Ama had lost because he had seen the massacre through his own eyes. He was eager to inflict punishment upon them for their wrong deeds. While he moved, he held the spear as tight as he could, expecting to be attacked by a slayer on the way. But, they seemed to have left the town and moved elsewhere. Soon, he reached the citadel and met the priest just before his death. He said before taking his last breath,

"They are Aryans. Do you hear me? They are Aryans..."
Ama nodded.
"Listen, my boy, the slayers who did massacre are Aryans."

The priest continued,
"I have a secret which I did not want the public to know about. I know who you really are. You are someone special. You are not an ordinary boy. You are here for a reason. That evening, it was your fortune that I

had FORETOLD. Seek your fortune in the Aryan camp. Great things are going to happen to you and your life, great things…"

He could not finish his words either. He closed his eyes, saying "great things!"

Ama, however, could not figure out what the priest meant by 'great things'. The sharp end of his spear shone brightly.

Ama followed the direction in which the Aryans had gone. He could see the footprints of a group of strange creatures. Those footprints were not of cows or camels. It was a different creature being taller and stronger than oxen. He had not seen such a creature being domesticated in any of the Harappan settlements earlier.

He walked continuously for hours. Even when he slept, he did not place the spear aside. His eyes showed how intense his revenge was. The stars above his head twinkled as he fell asleep.

As the night advanced, a cold gale blew across the grasslands of Daro where Ama was deep asleep. This chilled his body and sent electric waves down his spines.

Ama woke up and looked around as he held the spear in his hand. Ama recalled, perhaps, that 'East' was the direction in which he should traverse. Although it was the case, he wanted to get to know the slayers, who massacred his family, townsmen and peer group. He planned to see them once, before going to the Gangetic plains of the east. One or the other day, they would be punished, justice would be upheld and peace be brought back. Thus, revenge would be achieved by any means; he assumed this notion as he walked. Punishment was certain for the slayers, no matter how long it would take. Ama did not really know how long it would take for him to find the slayers. Moreover, he did not know what they looked like.

In spite of these many facts, Ama followed the foot prints of four legged strange creatures. That was not the only clue which could be seen on the way, but he could also see blood. He could see it all through his way, until then.

He stopped by a lake and drank as much water as possible before heading to the foothills of the mountain that came his way, which he believed to be impossible to surpass by mankind. Then, he remembered how traders from distant lands used to traverse to and fro, irrespective of the type of terrain. Those traders were immensely powerful. They could cross the mighty mountains of the North. If traders could do it, slayers could do it as well. So his notion, to say the least, confused him to a great extent. He wished they hadn't gone too far. He prayed fervently and saluted the Sun above his head, which had risen just then.

ᨀᨇ

CHAPTER III

By this time, Ama had already traveled several miles on foot. He had walked constantly for hours, only with a single aim of punishing the Aryans.

Suddenly he could feel sort of dust revolving around him in the air. He wondered intriguingly where the dust had come from. He recalled the night of death in Daro, which had experienced a somewhat similar kind of dusty wind prior to the massacre. When this idea came to his mind, Ama's blood boiled and anger flamed in his bosom. He held his spear tighter and looked around.

To the east, there was a camp, not too far from the place where he stood, having the indication of a large number of people living in it. Ama gazed at it for long. He could see the four legged creatures wandering here and there, in the vast grassland, which made him certain that he had reached the right place in right time.

Exactly then, a strange thought rose in his mind. They were many in number. They had countless armament. Ama could kill only one at a time, as he was not more than ten years old. Moreover, he did not know how to use a spear. He knew it could make anyone its victim if it was properly inserted into one's body. With this little knowledge, he had to fight thousands of strategic warriors in the Aryan camp. How on earth was a thirteen year old Ama going to do it? This new realization filled him with despair.

Darkness filled his heart. All his spirit flew out. For a moment, the dream of gaining victory over Aryans seemed like a mirage. This time, he felt like giving up. But giving up was of no use because there was no one waiting for him back home. He had lost his mother, father, friends and townsmen. If he gave up, would anyone appreciate him? If he didn't give up, would anyone care or was there anyone left to care? Ama had lost everyone. Not a single person, even of his acquaintance, was alive. Then why should he bother to fight Aryans? There was a strong reason. His dream was not only to inflict damage to Aryans, but also to re-establish peace in the valley of Indus. If he died in the process of fighting Aryans, who would re-establish peace in the valley of Indus? To re-establish peace, he must live longer. If he wanted to live longer, he had to drop the idea of attacking them, for the time being; so did he.

He was not content with this decision; but having now more courage, and consequently more curiosity, he moved towards the Aryan camp.

As he came nearer, he saw the working class people who were washing the cloths by the river. They were taller and had paler skin than the Harappans he was familiar with. The very first sight of Aryans disappointed Ama, because they did not match his perception of slayers. He had always imagined 'slayers' to be fiercer in appearance with bulgy eyes, two horns, and sharpened long nails, and so on. But these people looked friendlier and calm. How could these people ever kill any being? He filed to understand. He could not believe the fact that these people massacred his town overnight. While Ama was thinking over this and many other things, he did not realize he had already entered their boundary.

"Stop where you are! Don't you move!" It was a cautionary order.

An Aryan soldier's sharp-end sword touched his neck, moved vertically above his chin and pointed his frightened eyes.

"Who are you?" He questioned seriously.

"Ama" was the reply.

"Ama? Where do you come from?"

"Some slayers murdered my family, townsmen and plundered my town."

"Down the valley?"

Ama nodded his head in agreement.

"We are responsible for it, you little rat! How dare you call us slayers?"

He pushed Ama aside in bursting rage. Ama fell down to the ground and as a result, got injured on his limbs. When he tried to stand up, he could see a well-dressed, tall, authoritative mannered, middle-aged man before him. Everybody bent, saluted and addressed him as the Commander-in-chief.

"Who is this, Rana?" the commander questioned the man who had pushed Ama.

Rana bent and answered in a lowered tone,

"He is a boy from the Harappan town. I thought we had killed all. Permit me now; I'll make him forget he was alive."

His voice shook. The commander stared at Rana unhappily.

"No, let him go. He is only a child. What harm can he cause to us?"

The commander said thoughtfully. A moment later, he changed his mind and declared,

"This boy will stay with us. Yes, he won't go anywhere."

"Commander, I think you should reconsider your order," Rana said, fear in his voice was clear.

The commander unsheathed his sword,

"Who is the Commander-in-chief? You or me?"

"Commander, look at him. He has a spear with him."

"Never mind. Are you afraid of a spear? Do you think he can kill us with a spear?" He laughed and added, "He looks innocent. Let him play with our children."

He patted Ama's back and let him go. Ama was surprised by his attitude.

Looking at this, Rana muttered to himself,
"You will regret this, General."

Ama walked further searching for children of his age. On the river bank, a few children were playing. Ama went there and sat by them.

Hours passed. They continued playing and Ama continued watching them play. None of them called Ama to join them, nor did Ama beg them to include him in their group. In the midst of this, Ama saw a girl sitting on the grass all alone. Ama liked her peaceful appearance and went ahead to talk to her.

"I'm Ama," he said with a cute smile on his face.

She turned her face towards him to see who had come. Her eyes sparkled when she saw him. Those were not just eyes, but two gems. Her blue eyes shone in overwhelming joy. Ama looked in her eyes, quickly, and fell absolutely and everlastingly in love at first sight with the girl, who was gazing at him in wide-eyed bewilderment.

"I'm Shalakha!" Her voice was sweeter than all the Songbirds Ama had ever heard, and all the Music ever played.

"Oh!" exclaimed Ama, struck speechless by her beauty.

"Are you alone?" Ama asked innocently.

"Yes. Nobody allows me to play. They say I'm a lucky girl. Do you see my eyes? They are blue in colour. They think that if they are not careful some harm may be done to my eyes while playing. And they fear I would hold them responsible for it. Tell me, why would I do that?"

"Yes, your eyes are so beautiful," Ama admitted.

"Will you play with me? Let us count the stars tonight!" She laughed as she said it. Ama grinned. Shalakha's glee was visible in her glowing eyes.

Weeks ran fast. Ama and Shalakha became very good friends. He started adoring her company from the bottom of his heart.

Shalakha was an intelligent girl of twelve. She was beautiful, quick and alert. She knew the art of 'horse riding'. By 'Horse', she referred to those four legged strange creatures of Ama's observation. Every evening, she used to read palm scripts, in which she said 'Vedas' had been written. Ama did not understand everything Shalakha talked about. Shalakha made him familiar with horses and taught him how to control them.

Aryan camp was fertile. Everyone used to work hard and get their daily food. In spite of that, they were leading a rural life. Ama could see how backward they still were. Ama advised the Commander, who was the acting King of the camp, on each and every issue. In the beginning, he used to ignore him, but later accepted him for granted.

At times, Shalakha wondered how he knew so much. Ama talked about the construction of drainage system, making of bricks and so on. There were times when the Commander himself would stand up and clap for Ama.

In the next three years, the Commander himself taught Ama how to use different weapons including the most sensitive war tactics. His intention was to make the boy an invincible warrior. Ama was quick in learning. He learnt the different tactics of defence and attack. The war strategies were also taught to Ama.

"These spear and sword are in fact demons that, whenever unsheathed, crave blood without regard to friend or foe."

The commander would always preach Ama.

Whatever it was, Ama regarded Aryan society to be much complex. The society was hierarchical in order, with priests on the top and servant class at the bottom. He had not seen such a system in his town. Ama heard that there was a king who ruled them from a particular place.

Under the care of Shalakha, Ama became more and more perfect. She looked after him all the time. In return, Ama also took special care about Shalakha. He followed her everywhere. They were as if their souls were one and only bodies were different. It was nothing more than a change in the way they lived their lives.

Shalakha, as Ama had reckoned earlier, possessed a very beautiful voice. She used to sing folk songs for him, every night after the dinner. Her eyes would glow every time she saw him with his spear, for Ama would never put down his spear, it was either in his hand or on his back.

However, all these months, one thing was constantly bothering him- his revenge. The more he wanted to detach himself from his vow, the more he would get attached to it.

One night, Ama and Shalakha were gazing at the starry sky. Shalakha questioned him about his mother all of a sudden.

"Ama, where is your mother?"

Tears welled up in Ama's eyes. He pointed his finger at *Polaris*.

"I don't understand riddles," she said, "You lost her?"

"I did not lose her. She was stolen from me," Ama's voice trembled. Shalakha continued to look at him. Ama looked around to see if anyone was overhearing their conversation, then leaned forward and spoke in a low tone,

"Your people killed my mother. They killed my father. They killed my happiness."

Ama could not continue. Shalakha was shocked to realize something she did not really know. There was a long silence.

"Then why did you come here?" She asked with her eyes wide open.

"To take revenge. I have vowed before my father."

"I thought you came here seeking my friendship," Shalakha said stoically. She added,

"You know what?"

"What?" Ama asked.

"Do you know our astrologer who foretells the fortune of our people? He had once foretold that my boy would come with a spear in his hand. He said that boy would make my life worth living. When I met you, I thought it was you. But, I was wrong."

She stopped as her cheeks met with tears. Her gem-like eyes did not shine anymore.

"It is not so, Shalakha!"

"It is so, Ama. Don't tell me anything. You have come here to take revenge, to kill people. Say Yes or No?"

"Yes... But..." Ama admitted and tried to explain his point of view. She got up, wiped her eyes and ran away fighting to control her tears. Ama took a deep breath and said even though she had already left, "Shalakha, you know what? My fortune, too, had been foretold years ago. When my priest foretold my fortune, I did not realize it was something of this kind. You are my fortune. It's none other than you...I have realized this long back, when I met you for the first time, right here!"

He paused before telling,
"I love you, Shalakha!"
Two streams of tears gushed from his eyes and rolled down his cheeks.
"Tell me, do you love me?" He said looking at *Sirius*, the brightest star in the galaxy.

All night long, Ama sat beneath the starry sky thinking of his love, Shalakha. Ama placed a beautiful pearl on the rock that was beside. It was only then that he tasted the warm salty wetness of his own tears and realized how hard he was crying.

Just before the sunrise, a horse came in his direction, searching for food. Ama saw it and with a jump he was on horseback; before long, the horse disappeared in the darkness of the jungle, which was nearby.

A few birds began chirping as the Sun rose in the east. Shalakha, who had cried all night, came outside hoping to see Ama by the riverside. She wanted to let him know what she truly felt for him. Apparently, she loved him. She loved him more than anything. She had tried all night, to forget him and overcome his memories. She broke down many times in the process. She could not do it, not even once. Despite knowing the fact that he was there to kill her own people, she could not forget him. She could not even think of forgetting him. Ama was more than a friend for her, who had made a real difference in her life. She knew he was a special person in her little life and would be the only person to stand by her, no matter what. How could she ever hate him?

She came to the place where they had sat and chatted last night. Ama was not there. She could see the footprints of a horse running along the way to the forest. She clearly understood that Ama had left the camp.

"Why did you do this?" She questioned with two eyes full of tears.

"If this is what you wanted to do, why did you ever come into my life? You are a hero, Ama. Not a coward to run away like this."

She cried for long. She splashed the river water in overwhelming distress. She screamed,

"I love you, Ama. I love you so much. Do you hear me? Meeting again might not be possible. So listen to me, I love you and I mean it."

As she got up and turned, she found a pearl on the nearby rock. Looking at the pearl made her eyes shine more brightly than ever before. A smile appeared on her face.

"I know, Ama. You're a hero. I'll wait for you. But I will miss you!"

Saying this, she pressed the pearl to her lips.
She walked back into the shelter with a heavy heart.

The news spread like wildfire. But nobody could understand the reason why he had left. He had spent three meaningful springs with them and had now left them behind with his evergreen memories. Everyone in the Aryan camp was astonished by the sudden disappearance of Ama. They decided to wait for him. But when they saw that one of their horses was missing, they realized he would never come back.

"I told you, General. He was not Aryan to have trusted him so much," Rana said seriously.

"I knew he was not Aryan. But he was a human. In fact, he was one of the best human beings among us."

"You think he will return?"

"I don't just think so, I believe so," the commander ended the conversation.

Rana was highly unsatisfied with the way Ama was being treated. He always suspected non-Aryan people and believed that they were not trustworthy. He approached Shalakha to know where Ama had gone to.

"I don't know," Shalakha said facing the ground.

"You are lying," Rana shouted.

She shrugged, "May be."

"You will know when it happens - You will know the consequences of your lie."

Rana left her immediately without giving way to further communication. Shalakha viewed her pearl and smiled.

ಅಞ

CHAPTER IV

Ama rode for days. He kept on riding in the eastern direction. He crossed hills, mountains and several rivers. He traversed on the plains, slopes and through the thick forests. Ama was not afraid of anything; for he was ready to face everything. Ama had now brought his state of life to be much stronger in itself than it was at first, and much stronger to his mind, as well as to his body. He frequently thanked God for the infinite knowledge he could gain. He could easily defeat several men at a time, now. He had successfully digested various war tactics and 'how to defend' himself at any point of time. He moved ahead with vengeance.

'Am I ready to take my revenge?' was a question which he asked to himself, every now and then.

The beginning of Ama's journey was all the more perilous since the hot desert gave him more trouble than he had expected. It was so hot during the day that the horse refused to go faster. At nights, it was so cold that the horse, why, even Ama could not move ahead, anywhere.

However, as he moved further, he had to cross hills and rivers. The later part of the journey was no longer tough as it had been for days, until then.

It was at this point, Ama realized why the priest and his mother had suggested him to take the eastern route.

Ama moved further in the eastern direction until he reached the banks of the river Mahanadi. Before he could cross Mahanadi, he was attacked by a group of local tribes. Eight men surrounded him.

Ama carefully observed them, jumped in the air, turned his spear at a greater pace than he could have ever turned, and this at once made them surrender.

They sat on their knees and bowed before him.

"Where is your leader? Take me to him," Ama ordered them. Accordingly, he was taken before their leader. They told him how Ama freely floated in the air and defeated them, with special reference to his spear using skills. The leader seemed to have recognized his power. The leader, who had seen countless warriors over the years, quickly realized they were in danger. He told the rest of his men to surrender immediately.

"What do you want?" the leader asked him.

"You," Ama said pointing to the leader.

"What does that mean?"

"I need your people."

"What is the purpose? You need them as slaves?"

"No, certainly not. I want you to join me in my battle to re-establish peace in the Indus valley."

"What battle?"

"People who came from beyond the Northern Mountains destroyed my town, killed my people and plundered our wealth. I need your help to fight them. Be my ally."

Ama showed his hand as a sign of friendship. But the leader refused.

"This is your war. You want to kill our people? I don't agree. These people won't obey you."

"If I were to defeat and take your place?" Ama questioned raising his spear.

"Wait, let me think," he said without finding a way to convince him. Soon, he nodded his head in agreement. Ama promised permanent mutual co-operation in return. The tribes applauded.

"Are you leaving, Master?" the leader asked with exaggerated respect.

"Thousand men cannot battle them. They are trained warriors. I will be back with more men," Ama replied.

Ama rose quickly and set off further.

For two long years, Ama continued his conquest all over the Gangetic belt. He fought each and every tribal group in their own territory and inflicted crushing defeat upon them. Ama's military skills were amazing. He could fight any number of men with his spear.

Ama's territory went on extending day by day. More than thirty five tribal groups were under his control, and Ama was still not content with his strength. He desired to have even more. With his mighty force, he continued his expanse towards the eastern tip of the subcontinent.

Ama's conquests were subjected to the adding of his military force. He neither killed nor injured people; nor did he plunder the tribal villages. Wheat fields were left untouched; women, children and aged ones were not harmed at any point of time; but he forced every single man to join his army without fail. The expansion of Ama's army was much quicker than he, personally, could have anticipated. But there were many regrettable moments along the way. Dealings with the native tribes were dishonorable and a huge black mark that could not be denied. Ama knew what his faults were and all the occasions when his actions had gone wrong. But, his promise, however, was the only thing he could see before him and to an equal extent, his love, Shalakha. He would still think of her, even though it was much painful for him.

His entire trauma seemed irrational when her sparkling eyes appeared in the bottom of his heart. Those memories, which he could clearly recall, kept him in a state of dilemma. She was his fortune. There were occasions, despite his presently occupied activity, when Ama would have a feeling for loneliness.

Even though it was spring season, Ama could find only an autumn around. The beautiful songs of the birds, to his ears, sounded like mourning. The days began lingering. He could not experience a single moment of peace. Wherever he took rest, it was as if a brutal war had been going on for ages, both within and without.

However, Ama was well satisfied with his army now. He had a mighty army consisting of fifty thousand infantry, three thousand bamboo-made chariots, and fifty war elephants, which he had domesticated with the help of tribes. Ama had weapons like stone axes, poisoned spears, metal swords, discs and sharp stones. Those weapons were well polished soon after their preparation. Despite having so many diversified armaments, Ama preferred to use only his spear for himself, which he believed as his 'war winner'.

With the task of assembling Army accomplished, Ama wanted to win over his love. It was almost two years that he had been away from the place where he had seen her last. He was not quite sure where she was. But, with utmost hope, he traveled back on his horse to the same place.

While traveling back, he looked at *Sirius* and said,

"I'm coming Shalakha, to take you with me."

As a response, the star shone brightly. Ama smiled happily.

Little had changed in a year and half. Ama rode slowly, observing each and every phenomenon that took place in the environment. He faced numerous problems on his way back as well. At first, he faced a dusty wind from the west, probably caused by the sudden storm in the desert. It was a great obstacle as it made difficult for him to traverse any further.

Many more days later, Ama reached the land of the Indus valley civilization. By this time, Aryan settlements had grown larger with an area about half of the subcontinent, but the place where Ama had spent his three meaningful springs still remained as an important town in Aryan culture also.

As soon as it was night, Ama was on the riverbank, just in time.

To his surprise, Shalakha was standing there.

"I always knew," she said as she saw him get down from the horse back.

"What?"

"That you would return one or the other day," her eyes shone repeatedly.

"You know why I have returned?" Ama asked in amazement.

"I love you, Ama," she could not resist her tears coming out.

"I love you, Shalakha," Ama admitted.

As Shalakha came hurtling, Ama took her in his arms and hugged her tight. They hugged one another passionately. Dark, thick clouds covered the sky in order to prevent stars from seeing them. They remained in the same position for hours. Soon, the Sun gave signals of his arrival.

"Ama, take me with you," she said in a surrendering tone.

"I will," Ama smiled and took her hand in his.

"Allow me to look at my dear ones today, to my heart's content. I won't find them with me ever again!" She said painfully.

"Ah!" Ama expressed regret. He knew he was going to cause so much of pain and grief to his love, his fortune. But, he was determined, so was helpless.

"I don't blame you for that. I know what it is like to lose father and mother at the same time. So you have complete freedom to take your revenge, to fulfill your promises. I won't stop you. This is my promise!"

She said consoling Ama.

When she moved into the commander's house and touched his feet while he was deep asleep, Ama noticed overwhelming distress on her face. Having touched his feet, Shalakha came back, walked to another house and did her last greetings without making any noise.

Ama stood silent. Tears filled his eyes. He was deeply moved by Shalakha's love and affection towards her people. Shalakha came to him and for a while she was silent.

"Let us go, shall we? If they find us here, we may not be able to go, Ama."

Ama did not speak. He whistled his horse to come. They marched towards the east as quickly as possible.

All along the way, Shalakha was recalling her 'good gone days' with her beloved ones. She remembered how greatly she had been loved all those years. Everyone used to praise her, her eyes and beauty. But, every single civilian looked after her as if she was his own child.

Her parents had passed away long, long ago. Ama did not know this. She had told him that they were in another town. She placed Ama's love above all, above everything she admired, beyond everything and everyone she looked up to.

At last, she fell asleep on Ama's shoulder, while the horse continued to move on.

ಅ೮

CHAPTER V

Ama and Shalakha did not realize how the next fourteen months passed. In these fourteen months, they not only lived together, but also created memories for a lifetime. They sang, danced, walked, talked, cried, laughed and above all, loved one another unconditionally.

They shared everything in common except – philosophy for life. Ama's ultimate aim was to bring the Aryan race to an end, even knowing that Shalakha, his wife, was an Aryan. Killing the Aryans, from that aspect, would mean killing one or the other kin or kith of Shalakha.

Even though Shalakha led a happy life with Ama, her heart suffered grief thinking about the onset of a merciless war between her two ends, life partner and family respectively. Any result would cause her a considerable amount of pain. Shalakha had a strong belief in non-violence and peace, which she could not impose upon Ama, at anytime.

One night, Ama was sharpening the head of his spear. Shalakha was resting on his right shoulder.

"It's been months!" Shalakha uttered.

"How pleasant it has been!" remarked Ama.

Shalakha did not answer. She looked into his eyes steadily and intently.

"You want to tell me something, Shalakha?"

"Many things, Ama," she said caressing his hair.

"You want my absolute attention now?" asked Ama.

"I would enjoy having it," she replied with a grin.

Ama bent forward, kissed her forehead and whispered in her ears,

"I love you, Shalakha."

As a reaction, she smiled. Then, she spoke in a low tone,

"Actually I have a secret. So I'm bashful. Promise me one thing. I will tell you my secret."

Ama was surprised to see her shy-filled eyes and uncontrollable joy, which was visible on her face.

Ama nodded his head.

"Be with me, will you?" She asked with two eyes full of tears.

"I promise you," Ama placed her hand onto his lips.

"We are going to have a baby in six months," she said in delight.

Ama whooped as if he had realized all the happiness in the world. But to Shalakha's surprise, he did not stop sharpening his spear. He continued his activity without giving any interval.

"You don't feel happy?"

"Why? I'm so happy that I can hardly tell you anything!" Ama replied without stopping his activity.

"You are going to attack them next week, aren't you?" she asked stoically.

"How do you know that?" Ama became thoughtful.

"How could you conceal it from me? Did you think I would go and inform them in advance? Did you think I'm their spy? What do you think of me?"

Shalakha sobbed. Ama touched her gently and explained,

"You never say that again. You are my fortune. You have always been my fortune. I just did not want to make you upset. You think I will fail in my attempt?"

"I don't think so. You are not trying to understand. Do you realize, for how many centuries this war will repeat and cause more and more misery, just because of your one vow?

"What do you mean? You are telling me to withdraw?"

"Well, you punish them now. But we must all die one day. Then, they will punish our child tomorrow. You will not be there to protect him. Nobody is safe. Nobody is forever. Life is short, Ama. Let us make it sweet."

"Forgive me, Shalakha. Ask me anything. This has been my constant dream. I have sacrificed everything for this dream of mine."

Ama said firmly. On hearing this, tears ran down her cheeks.

"Ama, I feel like I don't know anything about you anymore. Will you promise me one more thing?"

"For sure!"

"Give a peaceful life to our child. This is my final prayer," her voice trembled.

Ama took a deep breath and said,

"I promise you, Shalakha. Our son will live in a peaceful land, where there will be no battles, no bloodshed or anything as such. This is my final battle. Whether I live or die, life in the Indus valley won't be the same again.

It will be refreshingly new, I promise you. Life in the Indus valley will never be the same again, believe me.

I will see that our son lives in a land where there is only peace.
There the wind will be fresh, as fresh as it was once. There, people will be free from all the harms, rich and happy by the blessings of the Mother Goddess. That is why I told you, Life in the Indus valley won't be the same again. And that's a promise."

Ama got up and walked to the army camp. Shalakha looked towards him with completely blank eyes.

Ama went on to examine the accuracy, quality and condition of his weapons. He knew what the war strategies of Aryans were. He had learnt most of them from the commander-in-chief of the Aryans. The same commander was going to be his opponent in the next ten days.

The commander was a tall and strong man, who had been dealing with armaments, wars and blood right from his childhood; He had been doing that for over four decades. Luckily, for Ama, he had turned compassionate.

The most crucial stage of Ama's life had come. It was not merely a battle for Ama; it was a penance of years. It was a penance to retrieve his lost land, pride and to fulfill his vow.

It had begun to snow about a week ago. Fat, wet flakes drifting down from a pale, pale sky started to slowly cover the forested ground all around. Ama shoved it away and held onto the branches of trees as he picked his way, slowly, down the side of the embankment.

His foot caught on a hidden tree root and he was sent tumbling a few feet. He caught himself against a tree and had the breath knocked out of him. He lay on the ground, panting for a moment, as the snow flurried down upon and around him. Picking himself up, his head rang and eyes swam. He must have knocked his head harder than he'd first thought.

He blinked downwards and was gladdened and relieved to see light glowing in a short distance. He had left his army there, two weeks ago. His men were busy practicing.

Having reached his destination, Ama began planning his attack. He divided his army into three sections viz infantry, chariots and guerilla. His war elephants were immensely powerful and could alter the result of the battle at any point of time. Aryans did not have elephants as did Ama, but a mighty cavalry.

Ama sketched the dispersed Aryan settlements of the west, marked the key spots which could help him get ahead and make his dream come true; spots such as bushy forests, small hills, deep valleys etc. were eventually selected and the army was arranged in such a way that even if he was destined to face the entire Aryan army, he would defeat them.

He instructed half of his infantry to attack from the eastern boundary of the Aryans, while the rest, he thought, should crush the Aryan army from the North. Guerillas were instructed to attack from the key spots, from more than three directions at a time. Chariots driven by donkeys and oxen were directed to follow Ama along with the half of his infantry that would attack the eastern boundary. Ama decided to start off on the next full moon, which was nine days from now. That night, Ama arranged special rituals and offered sacrifices to his deity, the Mother Goddess.

His burning desire became clearer, while to achieve it, he had to wait for nine more days.

ಶ್ರೀ

CHAPTER VI

After having his war strategies 'done', he ordered his army to begin their operation. He knew it would take nearly eight days to reach the boundaries of Aryan settlements. Shalakha stood still and dazed as Ama came closer seeking her inspiring words before leaving his territory.

'Why has God turned deaf to my prayers?' She thought painfully.

"I'm about to set off. Got anything to tell me?" Ama asked holding her arms passionately.

"Come back safely. Achieve victory. I know you will do it…"

She sighed with a forced smile.

"What makes you think so?"

"…because my Ama is a hero."

Ama stood by her, not speaking. Tears soaked his eyelash. And suddenly, from behind grey clouds, the sun came forth and shone with all his radiance paving the way for Ama to start about. Shalakha closed her eyes in complete desperation.

Ama hugged Shalakha as if it was for the final time and before she could react, deserted her. When she opened her eyes, Ama and his army, which was, for sometime, visible at a far distance, gradually disappeared from her sight. She wished that was not their last meet.

Shalakha sat on the same hill all day long, struggling with the dusty wind Ama had left behind. She was impatient to see Ama back home soon. She was not sure how long this war was going to last. Suddenly a mad fury gripped Shalakha. She feared what if her life ended while waiting for him.

Shalakha did not want to stay there anymore, for she wanted to follow him, as quickly as possible, to let him know that she wanted him back alive, even if he did not win the battle.

Soon, she readied another horse and followed the army as fast as she could.

The army was moving at a great pace. They were nearing a desert. From the great distance, they appeared like a large group of ants. Shalakha cried out Ama's name repeatedly. No one really heard Shalakha's loud cries. Even the strong wind blowing in the desert appeared to have no effect on them, as Shalakha stood motionless. The burning sun, apparently, was in favour of Ama, as He helped the army by reducing his radiance, to a considerable extent. The crazy climate of desert was unexpectedly new for the tribes and it was also helping in lifting their spirits to get a move on.

Although Shalakha tried to move faster, her horse restricted it, because it was really difficult to traverse on the desert all alone.

The army marched further and Shalakha was a day behind. Every morning, she would see them at a great distance; exactly then, her horse would demand rest and she would have to stop, even though she did not want to.

This persisted for eight days and seven nights. On the eighth night, the capital of Aryan settlement, where Ama had spent three years, witnessed a meteor shower. The horses began neighing feebly. The crops failed. Some parts of the river flooded, while the rest dried up all of a sudden. The dogs ran away madly. Earth quakes happened in some other Aryan settlements.

The Aryan astrologer got shocked by the sudden outrage of nature. At the same time, the commander called him down.

"What is happening?" asked the commander.

"The consequences," replied the astrologer calmly.

"Of what?"

"Remember, it has been more than half a decade. You massacred the town of Daro, didn't you?"

The commander did not speak.

"I had told you not to kill them. Should you have only conquered them, thousands of lives could have been saved. But you invaded the town, killed the men and plundered their wealth."

"I regret having done that, o holy one."

"It is of no use. You should have thought of it earlier. They were ardent followers of Mother Goddess. She will take Her revenge for killing Her children. As you sow, so shall you reap!"

"Is there nothing we can do about it? Will my sacrifice save my people?" The commander asked in a serious tone.

"Beg Her pardon. It will rain, even though it is winter, if She forgives you."

"Will it work?" He asked dubiously.

"Why not? Mother Goddess willing, it will happen!"

He smiled and closed his eyes. It was a clear indication that the astrologer had finished with him.

The commander now regretted more than he had ever done. It was purely an unintentional and 'not-preplanned' move from his side, the killing of more than five thousand men and women including their children. It was such a shame that he had realized something he should have actually realized before the massacre.

At last, he made up his mind to beg the pardon of the mighty Mother Goddess before the townsmen, soldiers and prisoners early in the morning. The news was announced and each and every one in the town was ordered to be present for the mass prayer.

Everyone in the town felt ashamed when they realized their mistake. The soldiers dropped their swords, sat motionless in overwhelming grief and shed tears for their sins.

ೞ

CHAPTER VII

It was midnight. Not everyone was asleep, though. Ama and the commander of his army, Bhola, a tribe from the Gangetic belt, were discussing about the battle that was hours away.

"Everyone in the town should be killed, that's all?" Bhola asked again in order to confirm the statement.

"Yes, Bhola," Ama patted his back letting go a deep sigh.

"What happened, Master? You look unwell."

"How many deaths? How much of bloodshed? I feel like I'm not human anymore."

"Master, are you giving up?" asked Bhola with his eyes wide open.

"No, not at all. But my vengeance is not as strong as it was once. I do not desire their deaths now. Do you know why?"
Bhola looked at his master in question.

"I'm dead, Bhola. I died long, long ago. I died during the process of becoming inhuman. I died with my parents. I died the moment I took this spear in my hand. I have died long, long ago."

"But revenge must be achieved by any means, Master."

"I can't," Ama mumbled.

"We will kill them, you order us. At least, their commander."

Saying this, Bhola went to sleep.

Ama's heart struggled to make a choice. His desire for revenge had almost died, now. The time that was spent with Shalakha had made him a kind creature, if not human being. He remembered his time in the Aryan camp, those three springs, which had been his golden springs; those three years had been the most active years of his life.

The dawn neared. But Ama shivered as he stepped further. He sat on the horseback as an idol in the sanctum. His spear faced the bare ground. The army marched directly towards the Aryan settlement.

Ama recalled his days with the Aryans, the love of each and every solider, the concern of the aged ones, and the affection of the younger ones; totally, it was the way they had treated him once, that changed the way Ama looked towards them.

There was no fire in Ama's heart now, but kindness. He replaced the revenge with love. The commander of the Aryan army was his guru, who taught him the basic lessons of war and weapons. How could he ever face his guru in the battlefield? And why would he ever do that? They were not his enemies, but his own people, with whom he had lived three years. If he was to kill them, the first to die would be the commander, his guru. The second person would be someone who, for sure, would have looked after Ama in one or the other way during his stay there. And the list went on likewise.

Before Ama could decide anything, they had reached the camp. Ama could not believe his eyes when he saw what was going on there.

The camp had been surrounded by a Chinese tribal group. The commander and others looked completely helpless as they sat on the knees, unable to move. It was apparent that they had been attacked. Bhola said,

"Master, this is a great opportunity. Give me the order. Let us join our hands with them. None of our soldiers will die."

"You're right. None of our soldiers should die."

Bhola did not understand the words of his Master. Ama signaled his army to attack the Chinese tribes.

Within a few minutes, a large number of soldiers and elephants attacked the Chinese tribes. This, however, was unexpected for both the tribes and Aryans.

Ama, himself, carried them along by force. Ama's mighty strength compelled the Chinese tribes to submit and to leave the boundaries of the Indus Valley immediately. Before they crossed a great distance, one of the Chinese tribes threw a poisonous arrow towards Ama, who was leading the defending army. The next moment, Ama was on the ground.

Nobody dared to see what happened to Ama. Moments later, the Aryan commander slowly walked to Ama and caressed his forehead. He wanted to see the face of the brave warrior who had saved the life of one and all.

"Ama?" He uttered in disbelief.

"I came here to kill you and your people, commander," Ama smiled softly to himself.

"Why did you save us, then? Why didn't you kill us?" The commander questioned. "It was so easy," he added.

"How could I have killed you? I have felt the same emotions, cherished the same values, and held the same things sacred for three prolonged years. For three springs, I have done that."

"I killed your family. I killed your townsmen. I killed everyone who belonged to you. I took away everything that belonged to you. Why do you show sympathy upon me? Why this unwanted mercy? Kill me before you die. I do not deserve your mercy."

"Can you bring my parents back to life?" Ama asked without paying heed to what he said.

"I admit it was a sin that I had committed. In fact, the biggest sin in the history one could have ever committed. I regret a lot. I regret, Ama."

"Do you really regret?" Ama asked in enduring pain.

"I wish I could go back and restart my life once again," the commander sobbed as he said it. He continued,

"Ama, I don't want you to forgive me. I want you to understand."

Ama smiled with great difficulty and replied,

"I forgive you."

The commander was unable to speak. Tears were flowing down his cheeks. He placed his sword on the ground and proclaimed,

"I surrender to you, Ama."

The moment he uttered it, rain came down in torrents. Both Aryan people and the tribes of Ama's army welcomed the proclamation. Beyond that, no one suggested doing anything. There was so obviously nothing to be done.

"Ama cannot be saved now," someone voiced his opinion.

"I don't want to be saved either," Ama rustled. As soon as he uttered those words, a solemn hush fell upon them- a silence so profound that they could hear their own hearts' beat.

A moment later, Ama looked around and as he had guessed, Shalakha was there, tired. She came hurtling into his arms. Her beautiful eyes were not shining anymore.

"Ama, please don't leave me all alone. Take me with you!"

She pleaded. Ama placed his head on her laps and spoke,

"Shalakha, you have been right all this time. If it weren't for my parent's death, I would have never held this spear. Believe it or not, I would have never even thought of doing all this.

My intention, however, is not to justify my actions. They can't be excused at all.

Today, although I did not kill a single warrior, although I did not make my 'Spear' bathe in blood as I had promised it, although I could not see my enemies falling helpless on the ground as I had dreamt it all these years, I have won the battle without really fighting it, without shedding even a single drop of blood. Yes, I have won this battle. I have won my land.

My mother was true, men rise and fall like winter crops. What remains is the name we achieve, which will be remembered throughout the time to come. It's not "what we make out of our lives", it's "how we live our lives" that matters the most.

At the end of our lives, we will not be judged by how many wars we have won, how much of land we have captured, or how many people we have killed. We will be judged by the number of good deeds we have done, because the one good life is the life that is lived for others. I now realize that the most important day of my life is still to come. Through my son, that is. Unfortunately, I couldn't realize it any sooner.

Teach our son the value and essence of peace and humanity. Tell him, once in a while, how his father lived and met his end.

There are so many things I want to tell my son, and right now, it is too late. I want my son to know who I am, what I have always believed in, and all the ways through which I have come to love him.

And finally,

I can't go away from you, Shalakha, my love. I'm right there in your heart, like an evergreen spring.

I'm with you forever, in the same place, like that bright star in the sky. You are not going to be alone, my love. You need to live for our son. I have kept my promise. He is going to live in a peaceful valley. And now, you should live to witness it.

But one guilt remains, have I given justice to my first promise? I promised you that I was going to be with you forever, yet I have lived only a short time with you. But we have created a lifetime memories, haven't we? All this time, I believe, I have loved you as best as I could.

I will always be with you...

A pause and then,

"Through my son..." he said, "I won't be GONE."

Shalakha did not respond. The very next moment, Ama broke his spear into two and expressed his final desire,

"Make your eyes shine once. Let me see it one last time before I die."

This time, Shalakha couldn't help shedding tears. How could she make her eyes shine when her husband was awaiting death right on her laps?

In spite of her deep depression, Shalakha made her eyes shine, for one last time, brighter than they had ever shone, for the man she had every truly loved. Ama closed his eyes saying,

"Give this broken spear to my son. So long, Farewell, my love! I love you."

"Oh, Ama! I love you!" echoed Shalakha in floods of tears.

The Indus valley had been the target of Ama for years, and finally, he had recovered it.

Five winters passed. It was the sixth winter in the valley of Indus. The heavy snow fall continued to dominate the valley for weeks. In the midst of this, Shalakha was preparing a woolen sweater for her son, Manu, who was playing nearby.

When she was finished with her work, she called him down and placed the sweater in his hand. Then, she told him to close his eyes, leaving the hands as they were. She transferred the broken spear to his hands. He was surprised to see what his Mother had just given him.

"Mother, why is this broken?"

"To save lives."

"Who broke this spear?"

"Your father."

"Why?"

"Because... Your father was a HERO."

They walked back to their shelter as the snow continued to fall.

ೞ౞

Bottom line

You have reached the last page of what you have been reading all along. This short fiction narrated you the fall of a small Harappan settlement and how a single person from that settlement bounced back. Within this context, we see how love and war change one's life.

There is a long established theory that Aryans were originally Middle Asians. In this short fiction, Ama (A Harappan) and Shalakha (An Aryan) marry and this leads to the rise of a new race. There is a reasonable amount of justice in assuming that whoever belonged to Harappan culture earlier might have come to be called Aryans later during the Vedic Period. Though there were two different races around 1800 BCE, we see the rise of Vedic period by 1500 BCE. Therefore, what I aim here to say is that at some point of time, Aryans must have found it beneficial to marry Harappan women, so they could settle down in the same places where Harappans had been living for millennia. By 1800 BCE, as it is narrated in this story, Aryan race had conquered one of the major towns of Harappan culture (The story does not speak about the fate of other towns). Ama, the sole survivor, then defeated them and paved way for a new race what may be termed as Indo- Aryan race. After the death of Ama, the still existing Aryan race flourished and occupied the Gangetic plains and lived a Vedic life, which is a later and well known phase in the history.

ಶುಭ

Taking it further (Suggested Reading)

Ancient Cities of the Indus Valley Civilization
by Jonathan Mark Kenoyer (American Institute of Pakistan Studies/Oxford, 1998)

Ancient India: Land of Mystery
Time-Life Lost Civilizations Series (1994)

Excavations at Harappa
Being an Account of Archaeological Excavations at Harappa carried out between the Years 1920-1921 and 1933-34 by Madhu Sarup Vats (1997 Reprint of 2 volumes first published in 1940.)

Excavations at Mohenjodaro, Pakistan, The Pottery:
With an Account of the Pottery from the 1950 Excavations of Sir Mortimer Wheeler by George Dales and Jonathan M. Kenoyer (Prehistory Press, 1991) - Two leading US archaeologists use pottery to probe some of the most valuable clues to the development of Indus Valley culture.

Forgotten Cities on the Indus
Edited by Jansen, Michael, Mulloy, Marie and Urban (Oxford Univ. Press, 1996)

The Indus Civilization
By Sir Mortimer Wheeler (Cambridge Univ. Press, 1962)

South Asian Archaeology 1989
Edited by Catharine Jarrige (Prehistory Press)

Post

Mr. Arun Kumar Pallathadka

418, Pallathadka, Perdala Via

Kasaragod, Kerala 671551

INDIA

Email

arunbharathiya@gmail.com

Facebook

www.facebook.com/Pallathadka

MoreBooks! publishing

i want morebooks!

Buy your books fast and straightforward online - at one of world's fastest growing online book stores! Environmentally sound due to Print-on-Demand technologies.

Buy your books online at
www.get-morebooks.com

Kaufen Sie Ihre Bücher schnell und unkompliziert online – auf einer der am schnellsten wachsenden Buchhandelsplattformen weltweit! Dank Print-On-Demand umwelt- und ressourcenschonend produziert.

Bücher schneller online kaufen
www.morebooks.de

VDM Verlagsservicegesellschaft mbH
Heinrich-Böcking-Str. 6-8   Telefon: +49 681 3720 174   info@vdm-vsg.de
D - 66121 Saarbrücken   Telefax: +49 681 3720 1749   www.vdm-vsg.de